Death

— and —

Other

Holidays

ALSO BY MARCI VOGEL

At the Corner of Wilshire & Nobody

Death

— *and* —

Other
Holidays

MARCI VOGEL

MELVILLE HOUSE
BROOKLYN · LONDON

DEATH AND OTHER HOLIDAYS

Melville House Publishing   Suite 2000
     46 John Street   and   16/18 Woodford Rd.
Brooklyn, NY 11201   London E7 0HA

mhpbooks.com
@melvillehouse

The manuscript for this book was previously selected as the winner of the inaugural Miami Book Fair / de Groot Prize for the Novella to which Melville House proudly serves as publishing partner. Miami Book Fair is a program of Miami Dade College.

Many thanks to the editors and readers of the following publications in which these sections first appeared, sometimes in slightly different versions: *Los Angeles Times Sunday Magazine*: "Go"; ¶ *A Magazine of Paragraphs*: "Heartbreak"; *Quarter After Eight*: "Physics for Poets"

A debt of gratitude as well to the thinkers, inventors, writers, and artists whose imaginations sparked my own. The epigraphs are from: "Return to Tipasa," *Lyrical and Critical Essays* by Albert Camus, edited by Philip Thody and translated by Ellen Conroy Kennedy; "Theses on the Philosophy of History," *Illuminations* by Walter Benjamin., edited by Hannah Arendt and translated by Leon Wieseltier.

ISBN: 978-1-61219-736-4
ISBN: 978-1-61219-737-1 (eBook)

Designed by Betty Lew

Printed in the United States of America

1 3 5 7 9 10 8 6 4 2

A catalog record for this book is available from the Library of Congress

For my mother, Ilene Estelle

The initial day of a calendar serves as a historical time-lapse camera. And, basically, it is the same day that keeps recurring in the guise of holidays, which are days of remembrance.

—WALTER BENJAMIN

In the depths of winter, I finally learned that within me there lay an invincible summer.

—ALBERT CAMUS

Contents

[1998–1999]

SPRING

Snap

I FOUND THIS OLD CAMERA when we were clearing out Wilson's dresser drawers, and I'm going to start taking pictures. Libby says I'm going to drive her crazy with all the snap, snap, snapping every two seconds, but I read about this woman in the newspaper. She said she's afraid of losing her mind, her memory, of being erased, so every day she takes a photograph of something, and that way she won't lose her life when the time comes. I thought it was a good idea.

Green

THEY SAY WINTER is the season of death, but anyone I've ever known who's died, they died in the spring. They say you're supposed to get this miraculous sense of renewal and promise, but it never happens that way, either. Libby says it's because we live in Los Angeles, and our seasonal clocks are set by new lipstick colors, but I don't think that's it. Maybe the changes aren't as obvious as in colder climates, but spring is spring, and it always feels kind of precarious. I mean, there's so much upheaval, all those blossoms forcing their way out of winter branches, tiny sprouts trying to break through the dirt. The whole business just seems a colossal effort, and if you don't have a pretty good reason for it, well, I guess I can understand why the entire scheme might not be worth another round.

Consider, for example, my father. He couldn't stand it, not one more spring. He hanged himself the year I turned sixteen. He left me his Datsun B210 hatchback, and it was months before I learned to operate the clutch without stalling. And my mother's mother, she held on all winter after a stroke. Halfway through March, she had enough. She made sure my mother knew how to cook a decent holiday brisket, then died in her sleep.

And now Wilson, my mother's second husband, Wilson, he died last week. I thought maybe he'd live forever, and maybe he would've if we had insisted on staying past visiting hours. He was so polite, he'd never die with us there. My mother called early Sunday, though, told me to meet her by the nurses' station. She took down all the get-well cards, tossed the dried-up flowers, his green striped pajamas, the slippers I got him last Father's Day. It was all done.

"Hey there, beauty, baby girl," he'd said. "Wilson's life is over now, yours is just beginning." He was pumped full of morphine and he wrote me this note: *Start, go.*

It was spring, and I knew he was right. I just didn't feel up to it was all.

Heartbreak

IT WAS THE FIRST new dress that Wilson wouldn't see, black with tiny white polka dots. "My husband died yesterday," my mother told the saleswoman as she rang up our purchase.

The first time my mother and Wilson saw each other was in that elegant Hollywood apartment, the one he shared with Leo Fine. They tell me I was busy crawling up the stairs one New Year's Eve when my mother shouted to Wilson, who was walking down, "Don't step on my baby!"

I was seven when they got married.

I never asked what happened in between.

Every spring, my mother and I would go shopping, we'd come home and take turns modeling new clothes, hats, shoes. My mother liked the skirts that twirled, she'd spin around, and Wilson would clap his hands and say, "Outta my mind over it! Best skirt in the world!" He'd have the Lakers on TV with the volume turned off, and if they missed a shot while we were changing in the next room, I'd know because I could hear his voice.

"Heartbreak," he'd say to no one in particular.

Balance

WILSON'S FAMILY WERE Petaluma poultry farmers, which is how Wilson learned to candle an egg, see if it was viable.

He showed me once how to balance an egg on its end during the spring equinox. He said it had something to do with the earth's axis, equal day and night or something. I tested it out for my sixth-grade science fair project and had nine eggs standing in a row on the new wood floor in the living room. My mother had just remodeled. She had a fit when I told her the eggs weren't hard-boiled. Wilson said they needed to be raw for it to work, but I found out later it was just a myth. Eggs will balance on any day of the year.

Vernal

IT WAS THE FRIDAY before Easter, but I drove over to pick up the ashes anyway because they'd already been sitting there a week, and I told the cremation lady I would. My mother told me she didn't want them at home. I told her not to worry, I'd pick them up.

It was far, so Libby went with me. We got lost like always, took a wrong exit. There was a guy dressed in a bunny suit standing on the corner, selling tulips. He held a blue umbrella because the fur on the costume was thick and it was a hot day.

I spotted a phone booth at the Shell station on the next corner. Libby pulled over, handed me a quarter, and I called the lady. She gave me the directions again, told me not to worry about being late. Back in the car it was hot, so we rolled the windows all the way down. Fumes from the traffic blew in.

Libby and I found the place, finally. It was nice inside, the walls a soothing shade of green. The reception area was furnished with two leather club chairs and a narrow antique table. A magenta gift bag sat on top, festive with a metallic sheen. The cremation lady walked in and whispered that it was Wilson, inside the bag. I signed some papers and Libby carried him out like we were going to a party.

Linger

I ALWAYS COME BACK FROM these big family events trailing half a dozen fragrances. Three I discern instantly from years of holidays with the aunts. Chanel No. 5 for Aunt Arlene, White Shoulders for Aunt Doris, and Shalimar for Aunt Estelle. All the rest blend together, except for my mother, who wears Wilson's favorite, Je Reviens, until it makes her too sad. She keeps an unopened bottle in her medicine chest, a circle of blue glass with a small gold cap.

It's a little disconcerting. I mean, you've just been to a wedding or Thanksgiving dinner, and you smell of everyone's scent but your own. I don't know what it is exactly, but everyone leaves a mark, so that whenever you touch your hand to your cheek, you're overcome with someone else for the day. Lipstick you can rub off, but perfume, perfume just stays.

Signature

WHEN WILSON WAS DYING in the hospital, I'd watch him sign his name over and over again in the air, *Ezra R. Wilson*. He'd hold an imaginary pen, a black Flair Paper Mate, start high at the left and boldly stroke down two round curves of the *E*. Sometimes he'd stop in the middle of his name, his brow dissatisfied with the motion his hand had taken. He'd start over again until the fast, sure lines cut through the air, just like they had always done on paper, *Ezra R. Wilson*.

My mother had wanted to take care of business, the lawyer had advised her, and she had Wilson signing all sorts of things. Checks, bills, car registrations, even thank-you cards to everyone who sent flower arrangements. In between documents, he'd practice to make sure he didn't lose his hand. He'd write his signature, and I'd watch.

Space

AFTER WILSON DIED, my mother started sleeping on his side of the bed so she wouldn't see the empty space where he used to be. He always took the left, like where your heart is inside your body, farthest from the door. It was late one Sunday morning when I walked in and saw her sleeping there.

Clasp

Passover, the aunts all go to Eden Cemetery to visit my grandmother. The spring Wilson died, my mother said she couldn't bear being around dead people, we drove to the desert to visit my uncle Joe instead. It was an obvious escape. Joe is my mother's only brother, the only one of my grandmother's five children who never married and who's always lived more than an hour's drive away.

After my grandfather died, my grandmother took turns living with each of her four daughters, carting her things around in brown paper grocery bags because a suitcase meant you were leaving home. Whenever she stayed with us, she'd sleep in my room, waking me up with her apnea or hypoxia, or whatever it is when you stop breathing at night. I'd lie still, listening hard through the dark, until there was a gasp and a sputtering, and the snoring would begin again.

My grandmother called Passover "Holiday," like it was the only one of the year. We never had a Seder, just the dinner, but it took a month for her to plan. She'd sit at the breakfast nook in our kitchen, clipping newspaper ads for brisket, making sure she got the best price for the best cut. There was always an argument because my mother insisted she was not about to drive halfway across the Valley to save ten cents on a five-pound piece of meat.

Unless the first night of Passover happens to fall on a

Sunday, we always get together the Sunday before or after it actually occurs. Uncle Joe still brings an elaborate basket of candy. When all the cousins were young, we even had an egg hunt. Until I was about nine, I thought we were celebrating Easter.

My grandmother would spend all morning in our kitchen, carving radish roses and seasoning the chicken liver she'd put through her grinder the night before, until my mother finally made her get dressed and gave my brother Jake five dollars to polish her fingernails so she wouldn't be able to do anything else. I'd bring all the bottled colors to the card table where she'd be sitting, waiting, fingers drumming.

She'd choose the brightest red, and Jake would paint it on, being careful not to smudge the skin around her nails, small-bedded and shaped like mine, only thicker and harder to cut. When he was finished, she'd fan out her fingers and wave her softly wrinkled hands through the air to make the lacquer dry faster. Jake would fasten her pearls, a lustrous double strand with a jeweled clasp. She kept them hidden in a tattered coin purse tucked inside the folds of her good dress.

The last time I saw her alive, it was in that care center, and her hands were bound in soft cloth like little cat's paws, the fingers all wrapped up in white cotton. My mother and I, we'd visit, and I'd sit next to her bed, thinking maybe that's why they used those mittens, to make it harder to hold on.

By Accident

UNCLE JOE LIVES ALONE on a golf course in a two-million-dollar house with country French decor, everything in blues and reds. None of the clocks work. There are three king-sized beds and four television sets.

I am driving to his house, and my mother is speculating about my uncle, who has been having some tests done lately because he doesn't seem to have any energy anymore.

"I think he'd be fine if he had a special lady friend," she says. "He needs something to look forward to."

While I am driving and my mother is rearranging my uncle's life, a Corvette speeds by suddenly, on my right. I stop at the light and glance in the rearview mirror. There is a family of birds, they look like quail, crossing the road. One of the fledglings has been hit, and a long line of traffic is forming behind.

"What is it?" my mother asks when she sees my face change.

"Don't look," I say, and she covers her eyes.

Museum Piece

I NEEDED TO GET BACK to work. Nearly all my vacation and sick days had been taken up with Wilson's dying, and I couldn't afford any more time away. Luckily, I rarely get sick, and I wasn't planning on going anywhere soon.

I'm a curatorial assistant at the county museum, which sounds more glamorous than it is. An assistant is an assistant, you do what others want. Libby says I'm wasting my life, but it hasn't been that long, and they give regular raises. Besides, I'm a public employee, so I get all holidays off, paid.

I'm almost always done by six, and on my lunch, I take a walk around the park, look at the tar pits, all the dinosaurs stuck in the black, sticky ooze. Sometimes I wander into the antiquities room, everything protected under glass, silent as a tomb. Whenever we show something big—Picasso, the Impressionists, van Gogh—the new galleries get jammed full of people. I prefer the permanent exhibitions, where nothing's changed since I was a girl, displays I used to visit, weekends with my father.

Dress Rehearsal

L IBBY AND I WENT searching for a wedding dress. She and Hugo are getting married next March, and all the magazines say you need at least nine months, if not more, to assure a perfect fit.

The first shop was called Cupid's Playground, and there must've been five thousand gowns, all zipped into clear plastic bags, looking like bodies in shrouds. The place was way out in the West Valley, and there were mannequins and mirrors and a swarm of bridal consultants, all running around in platform heels and lots of hair spray. In the middle of the fitting-room suite, a young woman modeled an ornate beaded ball gown for her mother. She wore a rhinestone tiara. An older man sat, tired in an overstuffed chair, nodding to whatever his small, neat wife requested in a determined staccato voice.

A fitter named Amber led us to our room. Libby stood on a raised pedestal, motionless and corseted, while Amber, ready in the corner, skipped a few steps to gain forward momentum, then flipped gown after gown over Libby's head. It was not a job for a weak constitution. I folded my legs atop a small brocade love seat and signaled *yes* or *no*, as was my assignment.

We didn't find anything worth buying that day, but I told Libby not to worry, there was still plenty of time.

Crash

I BROKE UP WITH MY boyfriend finally. He kept falling asleep on long drives.

"I'm sorry," he said. "It's the road, the monotony. I get hypnotized by the white line at the side of the road."

I wanted to shake him. It was as if he didn't care if he crashed, if we both crashed. Crash Man, I called him. We'd been seeing each other for months, and every time we got in the car, I ended up exhausted. I either had to do all the driving myself or silently clench my teeth in the passenger seat, watching that he didn't waver off the road.

We were on our way to Marin County, to Libby and Hugo's engagement party, headed north on Highway 5 just past the Grapevine, when I drove away. I left him at a Denny's. It wasn't nice, but I couldn't stand it anymore, being so close to someone who couldn't stay awake.

I pulled in to the bed-and-breakfast just as it was getting dark. "Where's Steven?" Libby asked, meeting me out front.

"Out. He needed a cup of coffee."

"Well, don't forget your lights," she said. "They're on."

Fortune

THE PARTY WAS AT Libby's parents' house in Corte Madera. They'd hired a fortune-teller for the occasion, inside a tent on the back deck. You went in, sat down, and she told you whatever you wanted to know. Or whatever she suspected you wanted to hear, which is maybe the same thing as far as divination goes.

When it was my turn, she asked if I'd ever had my cards read, and I told her about the Irish psychic who once predicted a small family of five.

Everybody's got a story, I guess. A clairvoyant's talent is figuring it out before you do. I've got this picture of my grandmother taken around the time of her engagement, and whenever I look at it, I'm surprised at how much bigger she seems, her strong arms, her round face. My grandmother, certainly, but looking so much like me, it makes me wonder how my arms will look after fifty years.

I bought this book once on how to read the future. THE SECRETS OF PERSONAL FULFILLMENT ARE IN THE PALM OF YOUR HAND. That's what was written on the back cover, anyway. It ended up being a lot more complicated. For one thing, I couldn't decide if my fingertips were square, conic, or spatulate, and the only distinguishing mark I could make out was a big gap in the middle of my head line, which probably means some future brain injury or something.

The woman in the tent turned out to be more spiritual advisor than fortune-teller. She didn't have any tragic news about my head, but she didn't seem too enthused either, especially considering the engagement party setting and the fact that I'm supposed to have my whole life ahead of me. She said this was not the year to talk about marriage. That, and I should take care to avoid precipices of any kind.

Vocal

I T SEEMS LIKE YESTERDAY Wilson and I were at ages where we both knew everything. It made it hard sometimes to have a regular conversation.

"Don't ever buy bread on a Wednesday," he'd warn. "That's the delivery guy's day off, the bread's not fresh." He knew this because he'd driven a bread truck for San Francisco Sourdough way back when.

"I've been alive fifty-three years, April," he'd say. "Do you know how long that is? More than half a century."

He was always so calm.

I was sixteen, so I'd get upset. Scream and yell about whales, flag burning, the president. I never argued unless I was sure I was right. These days, I keep my mouth shut.

Aunt Arlene, she's just the opposite. "I used to say nothing," she says, "sit around, feel sorry for myself. No more. If I'm upset, everyone knows it." She tells me this story:

"That doctor of Wilson's, Mr. Know-It-All, I called him up, I yelled in his ear for half an hour. *Who are you*, I says, *to tell a man, without his family there, without his wife, he's going to die this week? Let me tell you something, Doctor*, I says, *you may know about cancer and ureters and renal failure, but next time you decide to play god, just remember me— ramming your ass.* I hung up in his ear."

My mouth was wide open. "Wow," I said. "Good for you, Aunt Arlene."

"You should try it sometime," she said.

"Okay," I said. "I will."

Anchor

LIBBY AND HUGO BOUGHT a fixer-upper in the Valley, and I rented the one-bedroom downstairs from our old apartment. Except for my bed and dresser, all the furniture had been Libby's. Things were looking pretty bare, so I bought this little pine shelf to hold candlesticks, salt and pepper shakers, homey things I didn't even have. When I pounded in the first nail, the drywall crumbled underneath the hammer.

I called my mother's cousin, one of the Joes. There are about six or seven people in my family with the name of Joe, all named after my mother's uncle, who was a printer and who died before I was born. I was supposed to be Jody, but my father refused. I'm named after April, my father's sister and the only aunt I never met. She died when she was young, of scarlet fever, they really died of those things back then. That's why I'm April, even though I wasn't born until September.

The Joe I called is a retired machinist.

"You've got a drywall," he says. "Get yourself some anchors from the hardware store. You got a hardware store around there?" I told him I thought we had them in Mar Vista.

"Alrighty," he says. "First, put in your anchor. Make a

little hole to get it started. Then hammer in your nail, and you're set."

It took me a while to get to the hardware store down the street. The shelf sat on my floor for weeks, and every guy who came into the apartment had some advice for free. The building manager and cable hookup guy both tried knocking on the wall for studs. Hugo and my brother, Jake, also named for Joe, told me to get some toggle bolts. When I finally got to the hardware store, the clerk gave me a whole rundown on how to use the anchors. I listened like I hadn't heard it all before.

The anchors worked. I put the thing up myself.

Optics

I NEEDED MY VISION CHECKED. It wasn't like I'd heard, objects appearing unclear, it was more like my eyes were growing tired, it seemed all I wanted to do was close them, take a nap, especially when I was doing close-up work, really paying attention.

"Go to Leo Fine," my mother said. "His younger son's working with him now. They make a good living, optometrists."

It turns out Fine & Fine is on the approved providers list, so I make an appointment.

"Who referred you?" asks the receptionist when I walk into the office.

"Her mother," answers Leo, entering from the back examining rooms. He looks surprisingly official in a white coat. "April," he greets me, "you're the picture of Lena. You must hear that all the time."

"More than once," I say, following him past a display case of designer frames.

"We were so sorry to hear about Ezra. Please," he says, "have a seat." Leo motions me into a high black chair, swings a big machine with two empty holes in front of my face. "Look here," he directs, flashing blurry letters onto a screen. When the letters begin to solidify, he flips through a series of lenses and asks me to read what I see.

"It's too bad James isn't here," he remarks as I call out letters on the eye chart. "His fiancée's parents needed a lift to LAX. Remind me to give you their new number, I'm sure they'd love to get together."

He pulls out another instrument, asks me to steady my chin against a metal rest, then shines a sliver of light into my eyes. "This gives an amazing view," he says, and I wonder what else he can see.

"One more test, and we're through. Keep very still," he cautions, aiming a sharp puff of air into each eye. I barely blink.

Leo rolls the equipment away, pulls a notepad and pen from his pocket. "The problem is farsightedness. It's a minor correction. I can write a prescription, but with such slight astigmatism, lenses are a trade-off," he explains, drawing a diagram to show why everything in the distance will blur once I put on glasses.

Drive

MY MOTHER'S COUSIN JOE, not the fix-it Joe, the law-yer, wants to see me married to an honest, depend-able type, well employed with potential. Live in the suburbs, drive a Volvo station wagon like each of his twin daughters. I tell him the three dependable guys I've dated were dirt-poor and the ones with promising careers were also good liars, but Joe still keeps trying to set me up with the sons of partners in his firm.

I actually said yes, a couple of years ago after a breakup. He was already clerking, a bright Volvo future ahead of him, and what was wrong with me, I hated the way his mouth tasted.

We'd been going out about a month, and of course the whole family knew about it.

"Bring him to Holiday," my mother's voice rang through the phone.

"I don't want to make a big deal," I said.

"It's just us," she insisted.

"Fine," I said.

My brother, Jake, warned me there'd be expectations. "April," he said, calling on the sly, "why don't you ride with Emily and me? That way, you'll have an easy out." They picked me up in the Jetta, and we headed over to Aunt Arlene's.

Volvo Man showed up wearing a navy sport coat and

creased trousers. He brought supermarket Chardonnay and stargazer lilies, and won everybody over in about six seconds.

I took the wine and bouquet to the kitchen. Everything in there is white with little blue ducks, wallpaper, curtains, backsplash tiles. Aunt Arlene's been collecting for years, she's got duck-emblazoned pot holders, dessert molds, a graduated canister set. Even ceramic napkin rings, hand-painted with indigo feathers. I counted 168 ducks, not including the ones on the vase and corkscrew handle.

The aunts came in, finally, to plate the gefilte fish. They cornered me by the sideboard, stenciled with mallards. "You should learn to like him better," they scolded, but as soon as the dishes were cleared, I asked Jake and Emily to give me a lift home.

Libby still thinks any guy who drives a four-door is a good bet, but I think it's not the model so much as how someone handles the wheel. Wilson used to talk about this coupe he once owned, a 1956 Hudson Hornet. "I must've gotten a hundred dollars' worth of tickets in that car," he'd say. He always made it sound worth it.

Memorial

EVER SINCE WILSON DIED, I read the obituaries. He used to read them every day, I never asked why. He always read the entire newspaper, so it never seemed strange. He saved the comics for right before he went to sleep.

It started when I had to find a place that would do cremations. They have all these mortuary ads next to the funeral announcements in the newspaper, and while I'd wait for an undertaker to answer the phone, answer all my questions, I'd start reading the rest of the page, all the obituaries. Now it's a regular routine.

Every person's obituary has its own little story and whenever I read one, it feels solemn like a ceremony, and my mind starts composing silent elegies, something crazy like, *I know you now, even if it's only a little bit, and I know it's strange, but I didn't before, and I might never have known you, unless somebody had written these lines. Who knows how many people are missing you this very minute, late at night or early in the morning, drinking tea with milk, reading about the life you had, and wondering how are your loved ones doing?*

Bugs

ABOUT A MONTH AFTER I first left home, my left shin began to itch. I scratched it for a week until finally it swelled into a pale blue lump. Libby drove me to emergency. The doctor took out a long needle, told me it was okay if I screamed. He stuck it deep into my leg, drained out the infection. "You'll need to take antibiotics for ten days," he said. "Be sure to finish the prescription."

"It's probably one of those big spiders in that apartment of yours," Wilson told me. "They sit up on the ceiling, waiting for you to fall asleep."

"No insecticide," I insisted. "That stuff should be against the law."

This spring when Wilson was dying, the motion detector lights at the house stopped working. "I drove up and nothing," my mother said. Joe had the system disconnected and hooked up twice before figuring a bulb was burnt out. While he was at it, he installed an electric garage door opener, along with a timer for the porch lights. The lights come on automatically when it gets dark. This summer, my mother will look outside her window and see the moths flying around.

"You've got to get good habits," Wilson used to tell me. "Lock the screen doors at night. Keep out the bugs."

My habits have never been particularly good. I leave the

iron on all day, it used to drive Libby crazy. And I'm always locking my keys in the car. Wilson bought me a membership in the Auto Club because of this, and also because sometimes I forget to turn off my lights, especially if I've been driving at dusk. I've run down three batteries that way.

There aren't any screen doors at my new apartment, so I use this portable alarm Wilson gave me last winter. My mother said he walked up and down the mall searching for it. "He knew exactly what he wanted," she told me. The device has a flat metal piece that fits between the door and the jamb and screams at 120 decibels if an intruder tries to get in. It fits perfectly into my palm, and during the day, I hook it to my key chain. "There's a stainless steel ring you can pull if anyone attacks," Wilson had said.

Now that I was living alone, I was thinking about getting a bird, not some noisy, squawky bird, just another voice to welcome me home at night. A canary maybe. Libby and I had seen some vintage cages on Abbot Kinney, and a bird seemed easy enough. I went to the library, flipped through a book on care and feeding: *Sunset Easy Guide to Birds*. There were close-up photos showing eyes and beaks, claws being clipped. It looked as if you would have to hold the bird pretty close if you were going to groom it yourself. Another page showed pictures of possible diseases, birds with feathers matted together, parasites crawling around. I got to thinking maybe it wasn't such a good idea.

My new place is on the ground floor. It has an inefficient layout, but it was the only vacancy in the building, and right now it's just too much effort to move completely. At night, I jam a chair under the doorknob in case the alarm stops working and anyone tries to break in while I'm asleep. The first few nights, I kept the windows locked, until the air grew so stale, I decided it was worth the risk. Now the verticals click together whenever the breeze blows in, along with a low trumpet sound from the Swedish woman's husband a few doors down. He's a studio musician and practices every afternoon from eleven to three. They're expecting a baby in June.

It's not like I get a lot of calls, but the answering machine was Libby's, so I bought a new one. You never know who's going to want to talk to you while you're away. When Wilson was dying, I watched him dial my number one morning. He left me this message: "Hi, doll. I'm at the hospital. Give me a buzz when you get in, tell me what's happening." When I got home that night, I took the tape out so it wouldn't get erased. Sometimes I drop it in the new machine, push the play button, and listen to Wilson's voice.

The floor plan was never going to work, but I finally fixed up the new place. One of the Joes donated a matching couch and love seat, and I went to Ikea for lamps and a coffee table. I bought plants and pillows, hung up my paintings from art school. Libby said I should have a housewarming party, so I invited my mother, the aunts, Jake and Emily, a few neighbors, some people from work. I cooked for three days. The trumpet player, he brought a friend. Libby calls him Motorcycle Man. I shook his hand, took his leather jacket, his riding helmet. I showed him the pictures on my walls.

The next day, I caught a cold. My throat hurt, there was a tightness in my chest. I drove to Trader Joe's for tissues, orange juice, and chicken soup. I was back in my pajamas when the phone rang. I let the machine pick up. "Hey. It's me," an unfamiliar voice said. "Call me back when you can, okay? I'll take you for a spin on the Triumph."

Wilson used to tell me that love was like a fly in soup. "It comes when you least expect," he'd say whenever a date didn't work out. "That doesn't make it something you should necessarily eat," my mother would quip. She would have killed me if she found out I was riding on the back of a motorcycle, but I returned the call anyway.

After I got to feeling better, we went to an art-house movie, drove up Pacific Coast Highway for fish tacos. We passed by this little house in Santa Monica, on Twenty-First. He told me he'd wanted to rent it, but it was only available for a year. He said he wanted something more long-term. I pressed in close to his back, blinked my eyes against the wind. It was strange having someone stay at the new place. I didn't put the chair up under the knob or use the alarm. He left before dawn.

Later that morning, I baked some bread. I put the kettle on the fire, sprinkled yeast over lukewarm water. I opened the window to hear my neighbor practicing. The steam whistled, the yeast foamed, the trumpet blew.

SUMMER

Evolution

WE GET THESE BEETLES every summer, June bugs they're called, only they don't show up until July. Libby despises them.

"It's an infestation of idiocy, they zigzag aimlessly, bash into everything, and wind up flailing on the floor."

It's her pragmatic streak, I can't blame her protesting the inefficient. Even when we were in undergrad, Libby didn't waste time with unpaid internships or extra credit. She works downtown as a planner with the Department of Water and Power. She's the only woman on her team and already shares an office overlooking the 110 Freeway.

"At least they make decent dog entertainment," Hugo says. "Argos snaps at them until they fall on their backs. Then he paws them right-side up, and they fly away like they were never dead."

"That's what's so infuriating," Libby says. "They go against Darwin, these insects. It's like survival of the most unfit."

Libby's measure of truth can be exacting, but once she's a friend, it's forever.

List

I'M A LIST MAKER, my whole life, I've been a list maker. Not when things are going okay, no, when things are okay, I go with the flow. I forget where I'm supposed to be when, put off errands left and right. I sleep late and drink tea, read the paper until noon.

But when things are out of control, when I don't know what I'm doing, I make lists, detailed, prioritized lists. I write them on three-by-five cards, it keeps the tasks from getting too out of hand. Only about twenty will fit on one side. Any more than that and my head would explode from unfulfillable expectations, so I stick with a three-by-five card and twenty goals, numbered, organized. I stick the card in a flap in my purse, and I carry it all around town, to the supermarket, cleaners, bank, post office, crossing off all my to-do's. One Saturday morning, I got the car washed, the groceries bought, and my hair cut all before noon. It was an errand extravaganza. Big cross-off satisfaction.

By the time I've reached the last item, though, it's time to start over. The apartment needs to be cleaned, or the bills paid, or the laundry done. The dishes. And the milk. It's always expiring before I can finish the carton, and yet I always need more. It's the nature of milk, I guess. Libby says I would make a good TV commercial.

The end result is, I'm stuck with this endless, repeating

list. Sure, maybe there's a minute of satisfaction between everything being done and something needing to be done. Life doesn't rest, though. It's always slipping into the future, right when I was all caught up. It's always bringing me back into the thick of it, and I don't want to be in the thick of it. I want everything done.

Forecast

JUNE IN LOS ANGELES is not what people expect. June is overcast, and the closer you get to the beach, the more overcast it becomes. We call it June Gloom, but the technical term is a marine layer. It can start as early as May and stick around into the summer.

I'm no expert on the weather, but the coastal haze here has something to do with pressure systems, ocean currents, and an inversion of temperature. As the days heat up, the air closest to the surface of the Pacific gets trapped underneath the warmer layers above, until the sky becomes this big, white blur.

All the tourists complain, but it's not as if it's thunder and lightning, it won't strike out of nowhere. The problem is nobody bothers with sunscreen. It might not look sunny until noon, but you can still get a nasty burn.

Pale

I MET A FAMOUS RUSSIAN author once. I asked her about the sadness in her stories. "Bad things will happen to you in this life," she said, "don't worry about it too much."

It reminded me of this article I read about Moscow winters. Apparently, people get crazy with the lack of sunlight there in the winter months. The government pays millions for these artificial-light therapies, so the entire population won't kill themselves with vodka or whatever else. Everyone is walking around with tan bodies, like they've been vacationing in Hawaii. I live five miles from the beach, and my legs are white as a nun's.

"Maybe I should go to your salon," I tell Libby.

"You could use some color," she says. "Your legs look like Siberia."

"No," I say, "actually, they're all nice and tan up there. I read about it in the paper."

"Well, whatever. You need to build up a base for the summer. I'm booking us both appointments."

The next Saturday, I crawl into the tanning booth, lie on the smooth cool glass, pull the lid over my body, my eyes covered with little plastic cups.

"Nothing's happening," I call to Libby on the other side of the divider.

"You need to flick the switch," she says.

I do, and right away there's a humming and a buzzing, an orange light warming, until it gets increasingly hot so that I start sweating and worrying about skin cancer and if my time is almost up. I shut my eyes tight under their plastic shields, and it crosses my mind that the same sun that bronzes the body also hastens its death.

It's unbearably hot now, and I'm thinking maybe I should get out early when the whole thing shuts off with a lurch. There's a final, slight shake, and hours after I dress, I can still feel the heat, radiating underneath my clothes.

Patrimony

I USED TO HAVE two fathers, but now I have none. The first death was intended, he used a belt. The second one, Wilson, it was an accident of cells.

Sometimes, when I'd talk about my mother and Wilson, people would ask about my real father, and I'd say he died, and that was usually enough to end it. Some people, though, they want all the details. "So young," they remark. "Was he a heavy smoker?"

I used to say heart attack, but after I heard about aneurysms, I started using that, it sounded so plausible. There aren't a lot of details to fill in with an aneurysm.

Once, though, a woman asked me where it happened.

"His neck," I told her.

Things got quiet after that.

Tilt

IN *THE MAGIC MOUNTAIN*, Thomas Mann describes the astronomical phenomenon where, half the year, the northern hemisphere appears inclined toward life, the days stretching longer and longer until they reach their highest point of light, the summer solstice.

The calendar marks the day as the zenith of sunshine, but what's really happening is that from that point on, the North Pole begins moving farther and farther away from the sun, toward winter, and the darkest day of the year. It has to do with position. The moment your side of the planet reaches its peak, you're already headed into the night. It's one of those scientific facts everyone knows already, don't they?

Spark

FOURTH OF JULY WEEKEND, Libby and Hugo host a barbecue, their first party together at the new house. Libby surprised him with a new charcoal grill for the occasion, he doesn't trust propane.

I thought I might go with Motorcycle Man, but he called last minute, said he had to work overtime. I went anyway. Libby's parents were counting on me to take photos for the rehearsal dinner slide show, it was supposed to be a big surprise.

"Scarab," Libby said when she saw me drive up alone.

"It's fine," I lied.

Hugo's cousin, Victor, was back in town, and he brought a package of sparklers. He lit one and put it in my hand. I was surprised how pretty it was.

When I was little, we used to get together with the aunts, watch all the Joes put on a fireworks display. Now that the cousins are grown, they don't bother with the pyrotechnics. "Even if it was legal, it's much too dangerous," Aunt Estelle says. "That bottle rocket in Garden Grove, a hundred people lost their homes."

I shot two rolls of film and stayed through Hugo's watermelon skewers, then people started coupling up to make s'mores, so I grabbed my camera bag and told Libby I'd call her later.

"A player like that, I promise he won't last long," is all she says, walking me to the car.

My mother had wanted me to come by Aunt Arlene's, watch fireworks on TV, but I went back to the apartment instead, watched reruns of *I Love Lucy* to keep myself from dissolving.

Riverbed

MY APARTMENT IS a half-hour ride to the beach, and I never go. Libby's been lecturing me, she claims seawater is the surest antidote for heartbreak. "It's the salt, makes up for all the crying."

There's a bike path along Ballona Creek that leads straight to the ocean, but with all the rain this winter, the channel kept flooding. Now that it's dried out, my gears needed adjusting.

I would've called Joe, but I didn't want my mother to find out.

"I heard about that path on the news," she tells me. She's always hearing about bad paths on the news. "They attack you, take your money, take your bike. Thieves, rapists. You end up dead in the river."

"The river here is more like a concrete wash," I say.

"Don't be a wiseass," she says. "I heard about it on the news. Just don't go riding along that path."

She'd do anything for me not to die before she does.

Want

I WAS AT MY THERAPIST'S. I go Thursdays after work, my regular session since Libby suggested grief therapy might be a good idea.

"What do you want to say happened?" she asks today, not about Wilson but about my real father. When I don't say anything, she asks again.

"I want to say, *I wish he would have wanted to live.*"

She waits. When I don't say anything else she asks, "What if it wasn't a question of want, but of pain?"

Assemblage

LIBBY SAYS, IF ANYTHING, I think too much already, but lately I keep worrying about my brain. I seem to be having trouble speaking, finding the exact words I want to say. It's like the spiritual advisor told me, a big gap in my head line where the words should be.

Assembly line, for instance, the other day after reading about this performance artist who makes paintings like he's working in a factory, the same shape, the same color, row after row. He lays out a grid of small wood panels, twenty by twenty, then paints a circle of yellow in each corner until he's made four hundred suns. He dips his brush into blue, paints four hundred midnights, followed by four hundred swatches of green, four hundred white dots, four hundred strips of gray.

After the paintings are finished, the only way you can tell them apart is that he numbers each one across the bottom. *First* and *last*, though, he spells out the words.

Gut

A MAN AT THE GYM was working out with this fitness gadget exactly like one my father used to own. He used to roll it across the linoleum floor of our den. We'd be watching TV, and during commercials, my father would kneel down, take hold of either side of a handle intersecting a small black wheel, and roll out a set of twenty.

The man noticed me watching, and I told him I hadn't seen a roller like that since my father died. He said it strengthened the abs and offered me a try. He was right. You need a solid core to make it go.

He asked me how my father died, and when I said "He took his own life," surprising myself, the man told me his father had done the same.

So there we were, a son and a daughter of suicides, trying to keep our stomachs strong.

Hydroponic

HE TOLD ME HIS last name was Leaf, and he had this plantlike calm about him, so maybe I should have known.

"But what does he do, this . . . leaf?" my Swedish neighbor asks, her newborn baby girl cooing at her shoulder.

"He's an entrepreneur. Growth industries," I explain, repeating what he'd told me.

She purses her lips, glances at her husband, the trumpet player. He raises an eyebrow. They speak at exactly the same time.

"Drugs," they say.

I'd noticed him during my lunch breaks, strolling around the museum park in loose khakis, faded T-shirts, slipper-like shoes with thin rubber soles. He always looked caught outdoors by mistake, like maybe he'd just stepped onto the porch to get the morning paper and kept walking. By the time he asked me out, I was used to him, so I said okay.

He owned a Volvo, but not the dependable kind. It was a racy P1800, white with a red interior. Twice in one weekend, we ran out of gas, once right in the middle of Wilshire Boulevard.

He rented a large two-bedroom near the museum, and it had a peculiar odor, but I thought it was from the food.

He'd unhinged all the cabinet doors in the kitchen so that everything sat out in the open. It looked like a secondhand grocery store, used packages on display. "See, nothing to hide," he told me. Friday night, though, I flicked on the light switch to get a drink of water and saw about three thousand cockroaches scuttling across the chairs, the stove, the burners.

He was meticulous about nutrition. There was a chart on the refrigerator detailing optimal protein combinations and recommended intervals for eating. For two days, we consumed only eggs, toast, tofu, and a particular angel hair pasta from Trader Joe's.

It was Sunday, late afternoon, when he opened the closet in the spare bedroom. He'd just finished describing his dream house, a geodesic dome in the desert. Everything you'd ever need would be built in, delivered, or cultivated. There'd never be any reason to leave.

It was a whole setup. Recirculated water system, sprayers on timers, fertilizing trays, the healthiest plants I'd ever seen. I was impressed with the ingenuity.

Libby calls him Leaf Man, but what she doesn't know is what he told me about these connections in nature where possibility, probability, and reality are separated only by what people imagine to be true. "What we need to do is look behind everyday happenings, start seeing their real meanings," he told me. Some philosophy he called *The Transformation of Natural Properties*. I knew Libby was right, there was no future in a man who grew plants without soil, but I really did want to believe.

Regime

I ALWAYS ROMANTICIZE beauty treatments. Lavender massages, paraffin dips, European mud facials, every pore well tended and cleansed. I save money for weeks to indulge, but the truth is the pain always gets to me whenever I undergo anything more than a haircut, and sometimes even then.

"What's up with your forehead, April?" Libby asks when we meet for brunch, and she sends me to this aesthetician she swears by, Anka. "She's Ukrainian, she takes her work very seriously. Those Slavic women, their skin is clear no matter how bad things get."

It started okay, me relaxing under hot steam, until I felt a sharp pin dig into my cheek, forcing open a blemish. I clenched my fist tight, pressed a thumbnail deep into my palm to distract myself from the pain on my face. I made marks that stayed a week. Finally, I told Anka she'd better stop or I was going to pass out.

"The skin needs to be handled," she told me. "Some people, they are afraid of the skin. Myself, I am not afraid of the skin."

After all the redness went away, my complexion looked great, every inch radiant. I still had a few problem spots, but Libby says it was because I didn't let Anka finish her job properly.

Yesterday, Libby and I wandered into this little shop on Montana, where I fell in love with a slender silver bracelet, filigreed, very delicate. The saleswoman took it out of the case, and I slipped it over my wrist. "You could use a manicure," Libby said, noticing my uneven nails, but I lifted my hand to the light, heard myself say, "I'll take it."

Physics for Poets

WILSON TOLD ME ONCE that in every couple there's always one who loves the other just a little bit more. "Don't worry, April," he said, "you're the image of your mother. It won't be you."

I made sure to tell this to Math Man on our first date so he wouldn't make any wrong estimations. It's true my mother and I share the same face shape and sometimes, when I see photos of her at my age, it's like looking in a mirror. But the likeness ends there. My mother knows better than to take up with a man she can't live without.

Math Man solved equations for a living. He was taller than I am by almost a foot and a half, so sometimes when we kissed, I'd stand on the coffee table in my apartment to make up the difference.

Around the time we met, I was reading *A Brief History of Time* by Stephen Hawking, the famous physicist. Everybody thinks he won the Nobel Prize, but he didn't, I don't know why. In the book, Hawking explains how a star can get more and more compact until, finally, it collapses in on itself. If a star gets squashed like this, then it becomes a black hole, which means that anything passing by gets sucked into it forever.

The thing is, sometimes astronomers would see light that they thought was coming out of these black holes. What

Hawking proved was that this light doesn't come from inside the black hole, but from stuff on the outside, going in.

It's like this, I think: Sometimes atoms travel together in pairs through space. What happens when the coupled atoms pass by a black hole is that only one of them gets pulled in. The other is propelled in the opposite direction. At the exact moment of separation, there's a bright flash of light from the ripping apart. It's like the whole universe is shocked at the new arrangement.

This might not be exactly how it's explained in the book, but I've been thinking a lot about it lately because a week after Math Man and I slept together, one of my four-pearled earrings fell down the drain of my bathroom sink. It happened in an instant, dropped out of my hand, into the hole, and straight down the pipe. My mother had brought me the earrings from Hawaii. They were my favorite pair, the only fourteen-karat gold jewelry I owned.

I wasn't sure how to get the pipe off without a wrench, and it was too late to call anyone who would know, so I covered the sink with a towel to remind myself not to use the tap and went to the kitchen to brush my teeth.

The whole time I knew Math Man, which wasn't so very long, he was working on some complicated formula in which past information is used to make future predictions. If, for example, you knew someone's height and weight and a bunch of other details, like if they smoked or drank, you could predict that person's blood pressure. My guess is, if a person had unhealthy habits, their blood pressure probably wouldn't be very good, but Math Man's formula could give you exact numbers.

Math Man also talked about these chaos scientists who look at patterns and then make certain assumptions about how things work. His opinion was that such theorists are only making predictions about stuff that's already happened, but it seems to me if you're really paying attention, there's not much dividing what's happened from what's going to happen, or even from what might have happened, had things been different.

What I wonder is, if you could use these theories or ideas to predict how someone is going to act, how they're going to feel about a particular thing, a particular person. It seems to me if you could predict those things, you could save yourself a lot of grief.

My neighbor, the trumpet player, he unscrewed the drainpipe for me after work. We tried pulling the earring up with a bagless vacuum, but all we got were a couple of pieces of rust. He looked into the trap with a mirror and flashlight and said, "Don't be upset if it's not there, sweetheart." I told him not to bother putting the thing back together just yet.

The next day, I woke up around five a.m. and wandered into the bathroom. I got down on my knees and bowed my head in the small cabinet under the sink. I shined the flashlight into the trap. It was there, four tiny pearls held together in gold. I had a little square of gum left from the taqueria where Math Man and I had gone on our second date. I chewed it fast, stuck it on the end of my toothbrush, and picked up my treasure. The trumpet player put the pipe back together later.

FALL

Darkroom

There's this tiny closet in the apartment. I set it up as a darkroom, it's where I make my prints. It's a pretty straightforward process. You immerse the paper in a tray of fluid until an image appears, slowly at first, then all at once, as if you were recalling something you forgot. The next step stops the image developing further, until you transfer the paper into the solution that fixes it forever, makes it permanent on the page.

The part that always surprises me is after it's all done. The prints have been washed and dried, and I've taken them down, clip by clip, and I'm looking closely, really studying. It's a mystery how I could have been right there and have missed so much, in my mind, I mean, not the actual shot. The photos from Fourth of July, for instance. I remember taking close-ups of Libby and Hugo, the new grill on the patio, but there's also cut watermelon, confetti salad, Argos eyeing the burgers. And sitting over the pool—cross-legged atop the diving board—Hugo's cousin, Victor, in a halo of sparklers.

Fidelity

LIBBY SAYS I SHOULD GET a dog. She says it's a reliable means of assessment, walking a dog. "A man with a dog is a man who commits," she says. "Look at Hugo. Plus, it makes a great how-we-met story."

"But you met Hugo at a bar."

"Not exactly. It was an urban planning holiday party."

"Okay, but isn't Argos Victor's dog? I thought you guys were only taking care of him for a while."

"That's incidental. The point is, Hugo is forever."

"Fine, but you're forgetting one thing."

"What's that?"

"I'm afraid of them. Dogs, I mean. Remember that Rottweiler mix that used to roam all over campus, Dice? *Maybe I'll eat you, maybe I won't, just take your chances and roll.*"

Libby tells me I'm being ridiculous. "Off-leash dogs are not aggressors, April. It's only when they're in their own territory that there's any possibility of danger."

I remind her about that stray in the newspaper who wandered into a comatose woman's house and devoured her foot. "He was almost to the ankle before the daughter could fend him off, remember that?" I ask.

But she starts laughing, I can't believe it.

"A woman lost her foot," I say.

"For god's sake, April, she was almost dead. It's not like she's going to miss it. Anyway, you're not afraid of Argos."

"Argos has those sad brown eyes and heart-shaped ears. He's a keeper, it's different."

Center

WHEN I WAS A KID my feet turned in, and they thought ballet would fix it. I remember the teacher, her long legs and filmy pink skirt. She told us that when dancers spin, they pick a spot on the wall, and every time they turn, they immediately search out that spot again. They make of their bodies an axis, and fix their gaze over and over at the point of focus. It's how real dancers keep their balance, no matter how many times they twirl.

Quick Study

School's back in session, and the whole traffic pattern changes, so mornings I take a different route to the museum. My position is more administrative than educational, but sometimes when we're short on docents, I fill in for tours.

Back in high school, I had this boyfriend, Douglas, and all in all, he'd done a pretty good job for a kid. He used to carry around a big stack of books, even my heavy Gardner's *Art Through the Ages*. We met junior year after he got kicked out of prep school for not applying himself. He didn't do any better in public school, but he said at least they left him alone to read whatever he wanted. He was always reading something serious, philosophy or theology, or Dostoyevsky. He had a cat named Kierkegaard.

I've never been a great test taker, but Douglas helped me pass the AP lit exam. He'd picked up all these strategies at the private school and had a lot of time since he wasn't studying himself. I remember reading *The Plague* and trying to understand existentialism. Douglas said the readers for those standardized tests only scan for the basics, so I should just write whatever it said in the CliffsNotes, but they didn't really explain it except to say that eventually we are all going to die and, knowing this, we need to live each day as if it were the last.

Return

WE WERE AT EDEN to visit my grandmother. My mother wanted to skip it, but it was nearing the High Holidays, and the aunts guilted her into it. We ended up at the office, asking directions to her grave. The groundskeeper had worked there a long time, he was used to guiding lost relatives.

While he was tracking her down, I asked if he could look up my father. He was also buried there, but it had been years since the funeral, and I had no idea where to go.

The man located the correct plot in a big book and circled the area on a paper map. "Go down this path, see. Make a right, keep walking. It's four over, eight up. Not from the bottom, that'd make him in the Garden of Hebron and he's not there, he's in Jeremiah. Take this map, so as you don't pass it."

I took the map, you never know when you might need a map like that.

"Jeremiah's a bit of a trek," he warned, "especially on such a hot day. Just remember four over, eight up. Here, take one of these," he said, pressing a glass into my hand.

I looked to see the glass filled with white wax, a single wick in the center. "Yahrzeit," he explained. "For remembering."

"Thanks," I said.

The five of us started out. It was sweltering.

"Oy, it's hotter than hell," complained Aunt Arlene. "I'm dying."

"Shut up," said my mother. "Don't say that here."

———◆———

WE TRUDGED ALONG the road, and when we reached the sign that said Jeremiah, we started searching. We stepped around beloved mothers, grandmothers, great-grand-mothers. Dearest wives and daughters. We stepped around the fathers and the sons, brothers and sisters, rest peacefully eternal.

I spotted the plaque first.

The aunts and my mother came over to see.

"U.S. Navy?" said Aunt Estelle, puzzled. "In a Jewish cemetery?"

"It looks like he had no one, it looks like he was alone," said Aunt Doris.

"Oh my god, I'm never coming here with you again," said my mother.

I stared hard, pressed my lips tight, swallowed deep.

Rafael Goldring. 1932–1986. U.S. Navy.

"Okay, let's go," I said.

We were, all of us, quiet back to the car.

Later, I look up Jeremiah. I don't have a prayer book, so I use a dictionary: *A major Hebrew prophet of the sixth and seventh centuries. One who is pessimistic about the present and foresees a calamitous future.*

Just before the Days of Awe draw to a close, I light the glass yahrzeit candle like the groundskeeper told me. The whole cylinder glows. The next morning, I wake up to find the wick has gone out before all the wax has burned. I light the candle again, and this time the calendar pays no attention. The candle burns straight through into the next day, ordinary, holy.

Birthday Suit

EVERY SEVEN YEARS we become completely new people. I read about it in one of Libby's parents' magazines. Her parents always keep all these magazines on their den table, it's like the dentist's office, except for you don't have to get your teeth cleaned. Last time I was there, I was reading this article that explained how the body goes through this seven-year cycle where the cells completely regenerate themselves. From the time we're born until the time we die, we're constantly shedding old cells until we've got a whole new body, a whole new skin. I'm twenty-eight today, so I guess that means I'm starting over, fresh.

Seismic

IT WAS SOMETIME AFTER Labor Day. I was getting over Math Man, tall with a good job, half a dozen blue chamois shirts out of the J. Crew catalog, and a no-girlfriend policy. Libby set me up with someone she knew from publicity, his fiancée had broken it off a month into the engagement.

He reviewed films for a Hollywood circular. Our first date, he told me my furniture arrangement was dysfunctional. We were sitting on opposite ends of the couch after the movie, and there was nowhere to put his feet. "Most people put their coffee tables here," he said, pointing the tip of his Converse at the empty space. Critic Man, I called him.

"Thanks for the advice," I said.

"It's not like I don't have a coffee table," I told Libby the next day. "It's just if I put it in front of the couch, it blocks the front door."

"Forget it," she said.

I spent the next evening after work moving all the furniture around. I shoved the love seat opposite the couch and wedged the coffee table in the middle. Half the apartment was empty then because everything was crammed into one area, but I didn't know how to fix it, so I stopped and went to bed.

Around four in the morning, the earth started shaking. I ran naked to the doorway, crouched down, and covered my head with my hands. My organs felt as if they were swishing inside my body. After all was still, I looked in the living room and was startled to see everything so neatly rearranged in the darkness.

The phone lines were down most of the day, but Libby got through about noon. "I'm fine," I told her. "Everything's in a different place, but it looks a lot better this way."

She told me she was sending Hugo's cousin over to see if there was any invisible damage. "Victor knows about these things," she said. "He used to bolt foundations."

For the last couple of months, ever since he got back from Portland, Victor's been staying in Libby and Hugo's garage, where he builds furniture for people who can afford to hire designers. There's a studio off the backyard where he keeps his stuff, his clothes and books, but mostly, he lives in the garage with Argos and the sawdust. Inside the house, there are all these original pieces he's made, tilted book-cases, papier-mâchéd tables, three-legged chairs. It looks like a layout from a space-age bachelor pad magazine.

"What's with the names?" I asked Libby when he first arrived.

"Yeah, well, their grandfather worshiped Victor Hugo, it was his dying wish." She tells me they were born on the same day, two sons to two brothers, and the old man had insisted.

"It's a little weird, him staying with us," Libby says, "but there's no denying the guy's got skills. He's fixed every broken thing in the house, rebuilt half the kitchen, and he's only been here two months. Plus, we have all this fab furniture, at least until it gets shipped. Hugo adores him, and Victor's as loyal they come. He'd take out anyone who ever did Hugo wrong, even me, I bet."

"Everything seems fine," Victor said later that afternoon, taking a look around my apartment. "The furniture's a little crowded up in this one corner, but that's the way it goes with these dingbat units. Typical apartment space, it's hard to make the arrangement work. You'll be all right, though. You're safe."

"Thanks for coming by," I said.

"Easy done," he said. "Hey, do you want to grab a bite? That shaking was really something. I haven't eaten since yesterday."

"Sounds good," I said. "Let me get some cash. In case the credit card machines are down."

The only place that was open was the Japanese market on Centinela, so we stopped in and ordered udon at the food court. On the way out, we passed by the discount table, and I had just enough in my wallet to buy a set of four small bowls, stoneware with swirled centers.

Victor dropped me off in front of my building. "Thanks for the noodles," he said, leaning out the passenger-side window. "You were right about those ATMs."

"Sure thing," I said. "Say hi to Libby and Hugo."

"Let me know if you need help moving," he added, as if reading the future. "I'll bring the truck."

The next day I started looking for a new place. I don't know if it was the bad floor plan or the earthquake that made me decide, but it was time.

Yellow Tape

I FOUND A NEW APARTMENT pretty quick, a one-bedroom upper about a mile west. Victor came with his truck and moved me in about half an hour.

"Much better," he said, looking out the window and breathing in deep. "You can smell the ocean from here."

We walked to the corner store for sandwich fixings. All around there was bright yellow safety tape still up from the earthquake: CAUTION CAUTION CAUTION. We walked right on by them, and Victor told me about this project he worked on once, east of downtown.

"The houses were in a hundred-year flood zone, so they had to be raised four feet off the ground," he said. "It made for a steep climb to the front porch."

I imagined entire houses ripping apart from the ground, rolling down the street, out of the neighborhood.

The clerk rang up our stuff, and Victor took the bag. On the way back, we passed by a community garden. "Hey, look at that," Victor said, reaching for my hand. "Are you good at growing things?" he asked.

"I don't know," I said. "I never tried."

"Tomatoes are pretty easy to start. I can build you a trellis if you want."

I called Libby after he left.

"I don't know, April," she said. "Look, he's Hugo's family and in a few months he'll be mine, too, but I've been taking about five messages a day from some chick in Eugene and she's not exactly wishing him happy trails. Just be careful, okay?"

Bet

L EO FINE LIKES TO TELL the story of how my father placed his right hand palm down on a stack of cousin Joe's law books one night and swore he'd never get married.

"We'd get together for poker," Leo says, "all of us hitched and him free as a bird."

"What happened?" I ask one day.

"Your mother," Leo says. "He couldn't resist her."

Nine Lives

HALLOWEEN, MY MOTHER always bought the candy early. The whole month of October, we'd have to keep buying new bags because it would keep getting eaten. Now she says she can't be bothered. She puts out an empty bowl with a sign, *Take One*, turns out the lights, and goes to bed.

I didn't have any big plans, so when Libby asked if I'd come over to watch the house and pass out candy, I said I would. "There are a bajillion kids in this neighborhood and the yard is like a construction zone right now. Plus I'm worried about Argos. He can have a fierce bark."

"What about Victor?" I ask.

"He's been MIA all day. You'd be doing us a huge favor, April. Hugo and I can't get out of this client party, and I'd feel a lot more secure if someone was there. Stay the night, we'll go for brunch in the morning?"

"Of course," I tell her because an empty house is better than an empty apartment with no trick-or-treaters. Halloween evening, I dress in black, then drive by Rite Aid to pick up an extra bag of candy, a pair of fuzzy cat ears, and matching cat tail. By the time I get to the house, they've already left. Argos is whining at me from behind the back door. I let myself in, give him a quick scratch behind the ears, and he follows me to the bathroom, where I draw whiskers on my face with one of Libby's eyebrow pencils and arrange the cat ears on top of my head. I wave the cat tail at Argos. He wags back.

I can't find the stash of candy Libby says she's left in the kitchen, so I open my bag into a big Tupperware and take it out to the front porch. Someone is already there. I scream and drop the bowl. Fun-size bars scatter everywhere.

It's Victor. He stands up fast and switches on the outside light. He's wearing a tuxedo jacket and a white hockey mask covered with antique electrical parts. He looks like some nineteenth-century lab experiment. "April, what are you doing here?"

"Libby asked me to come by the house. She didn't think you were around," I say, still startled.

"Somebody needed to hand out treats," he answers. "There are a zillion kids in this neighborhood." And then, "I'm sorry I scared you, April. You make a good cat. Doesn't she, Argos?" Argos wags his tail. The costume one is in his mouth.

Victor takes off his mask and kisses me. My whiskers leave black streaks on his nose. Argos circles himself onto his blanket. We go inside, leave the candy and the bowl.

Counter

VICTOR CALLED AGAIN. He left a message on the machine. "Look, I know Libby's got her doubts about me, and maybe she has good reason. But I'd really like to see you again and explain. Call me back sometime?"

I lifted the receiver, dialed his number. "You don't owe me any explanations," I said through the line.

He picked me up in his truck, and we went to this ancient burger place Wilson used to take me to, Friday evenings on his way home from work, whenever my mother was out with the aunts.

The Apple Pan has been on Pico forever, a single room of linoleum and plaid, wood wainscoting, double-hung windows, and ceiling fans. There aren't any tables, just a big U-shaped counter with red stools all around. You wait on either the left or the right, until someone finishes and a seat opens up.

One waiter works each side of the counter. Wilson and I always ordered from the guy with a thick gold band on his left ring finger. It presses into his skin like he's been wearing it since he was a very young man. I went in once after Wilson died, and he served me this huge slice of banana cream pie. I'd never been in there alone.

I always order the Steakburger, which is really just a hamburger, I guess. I don't get cheese, only lettuce, and they don't have tomato, just ketchup, which I don't eat on the burger, only a little on my fries. I never drink coffee, but Wilson thought theirs was the best in town. Sometimes he wouldn't get anything except coffee with cream and a slice of apple pie.

Victor and I take seats on my usual side, and the waiter leans over the counter, nods at us, his ring glinting.

"Coffee, please," Victor says.

"You?"

"Sure," I say, "make it two." The man raises one eyebrow slightly, brings two coffees, two thimbles of thick cream. I pour mine into my cup and watch it rise to the top, spiraling like cool, white echoes.

Veteran

THERE ARE THESE LEGAL holidays you get only if you're a teacher or a postal worker or banker or some kind of county employee. The rest of the city goes about its business, and it feels a little strange, not working when everyone else is. I usually spend the day cleaning or doing laundry or something off the to-do list. These holidays are usually commemorative in nature, and I don't know, but I feel a certain obligation.

Wilson was a veteran, and he used to tell me this story about being on leave in Boston before shipping overseas. "Coldest place I've ever been. My buddy and I, we couldn't find dates to save our lives. And we were good-looking guys, too, in our uniforms."

This year turned out to be more of a sick day than a holiday. I forgot to turn off the alarm on the clock, and when it rang, my throat felt scratchy. I rinsed my face, brushed my teeth, dressed in a heavy sweater and jeans, and drove over to Trader Joe's for the usual orange juice, tissues, and chicken soup.

The parking lot was packed, everyone else must have also had the day off. They must have also been sick, because there was an empty space where the chicken soup should have been. A worker in a Hawaiian shirt walked by. "Sorry," he said, "we've been out all week. The tomato basil is good if you want to give it a try. Lots of vitamin C."

I reach for the tomato soup and wait my turn in a long line. The checkout guy asks how I am. "I've got a cold," I say.

"It sure is," he says. "It looks like rain."

I ask about the bandage on his left two fingers. "Playing basketball," he says, "jammed 'em."

"Sounds painful."

"Yeah, well. They're almost healed."

"Take it easy," I say, wheeling away my cart.

When I get home, I pour the soup into a saucepan and heat it up on the stove. Little black flecks float to the top. They look like flies at first, but then I remember about the basil.

I'm eating the soup at the coffee table when I see the light blinking on the answering machine. It's a message from Victor. "Hey, maybe you have the day off? Give me a call, maybe we can go hiking or something."

Swerve

WE ARE IN THE TRUCK on our way to Solstice Canyon, and I am staring at the middle of Victor's steering wheel, wondering why it's smashed in when he tells me he's the one who did it.

We reach the park entrance, and he parks the truck and we get out, and I say, "Okay, tell me more."

We start walking. Victor takes a breath. "I deal with depression," he says. "The serious kind. It's gotten pretty rough sometimes, Hugo can tell you how much. He's always been there to help. I take meds, see someone every week."

"What about Portland?" I ask.

"I signed up to build houses for people who had no place to live, so I went. It's done me good. I've been stable over a year."

"What about the woman in Eugene?"

"I haven't always made the best decisions, April. I'm working on it." He looks up. We're at the trailhead.

"Me, too," I say.

And because I don't want to love another man who kills himself, I ask Victor if he's ever tried.

"No," he says, taking my hand. "I promised Hugo I wouldn't."

We keep walking, and Victor continues. "I had a younger brother named James. Hugo used to stay with us summers.

The neighbors called us the Three Musketeers. The summer Hugo and I were eleven, James drowned. It was an accident. Argos started barking and dove in, it's how we found him. My parents split up afterward, but Hugo and I promised we'd stay in the world together, just the way we came in."

We reach the burned-down house with the stone foundation, the one by the creek. We wander up the trail and sit on a flat rock by the waterfall. Victor slips off his pack and hands me a Nalgene bottle. I take a deep swallow and pass it back to him.

Saturation

ABOUT A MONTH AFTER Wilson died, I was washing the Civic with an old V-neck T-shirt of his. It smelled of witch hazel and Vitalis. It soaked into my clothes, my hair, my teeth, into my bones.

"April, my love," he used to say, "the problems of the world are impossible to solve." I forgot to turn off the hose and got drenched.

Leap

Don't you believe he'll keep his word?" my therapist asks when I tell her the story about Victor's brother, the depression, his promise to Hugo.

I couldn't stop sobbing. She waited.

"Yes," I said finally. "It's myself I worry about."

"How do you mean?"

"How do I know it will last, that it's real?"

"That's love, April. You never know. You feel."

Harvest

I DON'T KNOW WHY I thought I could grow anything, but it seemed worth a go.

Victor told me I could sign up for a plot in the community garden down the street from my new apartment. It has a great view, you can see all the way to the ocean. I went to the nursery and bought all kinds of stuff. Gloves, seeds, fertilizer, an assortment of shovels and rakes. I put it all in the trunk of my car.

Victor and I took to walking over in the evenings, after dinner. The first time we went, Victor tore out all the weeds with his bare hands while I watched the sun go down. After that, it became our regular Friday night date. We kept a couple of aluminum and nylon-webbed folding chairs there. We'd sit them in the dirt, watch the pink sky, the glassy ocean.

The Friday after Thanksgiving, we actually drove over. We took all the gear out of the car, turned over the dirt, and emptied a bag of Soil Grow into the ground. The woman in the next plot told us it wasn't really the season to start a garden, not tomatoes, anyway. I looked up early-winter planting in a book I got from the library: *Sunset Easy Guide to Vegetable Gardens*. It said lettuce and certain kinds of beans.

"This is California," Victor said, "plant whatever you want."

I bought seeds for lettuce, zucchini, and green beans, and drove over to the garden. I followed the directions on the back of the seed packets, planted the zucchini in two lopsided circles, the beans in a small grid. They would need watering more than every Friday.

"It's best to come in the early morning or evening," the woman in the next plot told me. "If you're going to be here in the afternoons, you'll need a hat."

"Yeah, okay," I said. "Thanks."

About every two days, I drove over to the garden after work, put on my blue denim hat, and watered the dirt. By the next Friday, the beans had sprouted. I showed Victor.

"Beans put in the ground will do that," he said.

In another week or so, the zucchini plants poked up, and the beans were ready to pick. I cooked them that evening for dinner. We each got twelve beans.

Later, we walked over to the garden to see the bright orange flowers on the zucchini plants. It was getting dark early now, and the petals glowed like huge orange bugs in the twilight.

The next week, I had a big project at work, and by the following Friday, everything had wilted from no water. I was miserable with failure. Victor kissed me, held my hand all the way back to the apartment.

The next day, I got the yearly Jewish New Year's letter from Esther and Saul, elderly cousins of my father's. Three months late, the letter had been forwarded to my new place. It was written all in capital letters.

WHAT IS GOING ON IN OUR GARDEN: THINGS ARE NOT GOING TOO WELL. WE HAD SOME CABBAGE BUT IT TASTED BITTER; THE TOMATO PLANTS STARTED OUT VERY GOOD BUT BY THE TIME THE FRUIT CAME THE PLANTS WILTED SO IT COULD HAVE BEEN THE HEAT OR A FUNGUS IN THE SOIL. THE FIG TREE IS DOING VERY WELL EXCEPT THE GREEN FIGS THAT ARE SUPPOSED TO TASTE SWEET ARE NOT. WE ALWAYS HAVE A ROSE ON OUR DINING ROOM TABLE.

Diagram of Dogs

Victor's dog Argos was named after the dog in the *Odyssey*, which is what Victor was reading when he found him as a puppy, abandoned on the street. They'd been together a long time, Argos and Victor, eighteen years. Long before me. Long before any woman. Any girl, even. It was boys only for a long time, and they didn't mind, those boys.

Victor's Argos was a graceful chocolate Lab mix, with a deeply curved chest and majestic head. He stood as high as my hip and had a sly way of nudging underneath my hand so as to start me petting his ears, symmetrical, heart-shaped.

They lived in a little studio off Libby and Hugo's garage, where Victor made furniture for hours, shaping and sanding his imagination into tables and desks, cabinets and chairs. Argos spent most of his time sleeping on layers of cotton quilted moving blankets. Whenever I'd visit, he'd hobble over to wherever Victor and I were kissing and squeeze himself in between us, the oil from his fur turning whatever I was wearing brown. Victor's clothes would be brown already, stained with Argos and a fine layer of sawdust.

The workshop was jammed with stuff. There were piles of wood stacked on either side of the door, lumber thick as telephone poles, along with saws and machinery, all kinds of things I didn't know how to use, tools with sharp edges and unfamiliar names, jigs, jointers, clamps, and planes. Everything was dirty, dangerous, or noisy, and it all smelled of slightly damp brown fur.

If I was around when Victor was working one of the saws, he took care to wear protective goggles and big plastic ear covers that made him look as if he were ready to take off flying. Argos's hearing was nearly gone by then, the machines never bothered him.

Some nights, Victor drove to my place and left Argos asleep on the blankets. One evening, after we'd washed the dishes and curled up on the couch, he told me Argos was dying. "He's not eating, April. He falls down and can't get up without my helping him. I don't know what to do," he said, choking up. I said I'd find out, and Victor drove back so Argos wouldn't be alone.

The next day, I went to a vet's office we'd passed on the way to the garden. It had a dog's entrance and a cat's entrance, but I didn't have an animal with me and I wasn't sure what to do, so I just stood there. In the end, I chose the dog's entrance because I figured it was about a dog.

A receptionist greeted me. "How can I help you?" she asked, but when I tried to answer, no words came out.

"Oh, honey," she said. "I'm sorry." She motioned to a box of Kleenex on the counter, told me what to expect. We could stay in the room. It wouldn't take long. We'd need an appointment. She handed me a card. "Call when you're ready," she said.

Victor came over that night. "It's time," he said. I circled my arms around his shoulders and showed him the card with the vet's number. He called to make the appointment, and we left to be with Argos. We had until noon the next day.

We woke up early, but time passed quickly anyway. Argos always loved water, so Victor took him round back for a bath. I watched the brown coming off in his hands as he soaped Argos's coat. "Almost done, old man, almost done," Victor whispered, until the water from the hose ran clean. "Where's all the brown going to come from, Argos? Leather and wood and chocolate? Will there be any left when you're gone, source of all brown in the world?" Victor dried Argos's ears then, his hands gentle and sure, the way he handled wood, the way he touched me.

We lifted Argos into the truck bed lined with blankets and drove to Rancho Park. He ambled through the grass, then gnawed clean the bone we'd picked up at the butcher's. Finally, we drove to the vet, walked in the dog's entrance, and waited.

An assistant showed us to a small room with an examining table and a large wall chart of dog breeds. I counted seven main categories: working dogs, hounds, sporting dogs, terriers, toy dogs, non-sporting dogs, and herding. Each category was linked to another with connecting lines, it was like a whole blueprint of relationships.

I looked to see what it meant to be part German short-haired, part chocolate Lab. *Sporting. Half pointer, half retriever.*

When Victor was a boy, his brother drowned in the backyard pool they swam in every summer. It was Argos who dove in after him, barked so the others would follow.

In the bottom right-hand corner of the chart there was an illustration of a dog tag: *Diagram of Dogs*, it said. *Please return if lost.*

The vet came in then, told Victor they don't often come across dogs of Argos's size at eighteen years, told him he was sorry. "It's a lethal dose of barbiturates, it's painless, it'll be about fifteen seconds. You may see some movement in the ears or paws, it's only muscles reacting. I assure you, there won't be any pain."

Victor placed his hands on Argos. I placed my hands on Victor. When it was over, Victor removed Argos's collar, soft leather the exact color of his fur.

Back in the truck, Victor hooked the collar over the rear-view mirror, so that the tag hung suspended in the center of the windshield. The tag is a flat gold circle, like the tag in the diagram, only all the etching is worn away. Sometimes driving next to Victor, I look over, and it catches the light, like a low full moon, or maybe a midnight sun.

WINTER

Revolve

NOBODY EXPECTS to be cold in Los Angeles, but winter indoors can be freezing. Victor says it's because these old stucco buildings are constructed like Lego sets, no insulation or weather stripping.

Most people just crank up the heat for a few chilly weeks between Thanksgiving and New Year's. It drives Libby nuts. "It's as if the energy crisis never happened," she complains, but back when we shared a place, I'd sneak a turn on the thermostat dial whenever the temperature fell below sixty.

Now when Victor and I are asleep, and it's cold, I nestle close to him, until he gets too hot and inches away. In the middle of the night, he's always having to get out of bed and come around the other side because I keep moving to wherever he is until he's on the edge, about to fall off. I told him he should just push me over, but he says it's easier to just go around.

He says I'm like one of those heliotropic plants, a sunflower or black-eyed Susan. We saw a stand of them last time we went hiking in Solstice Canyon. Their centers weren't actually black, but dark dark brown, the same brown Argos was.

Shelter

VICTOR CAME WITH ME to Aunt Arlene's house. It's the largest house of all the aunts', she's got a whole room devoted to ships. There are dark, wood-paneled walls with fishing nets affixed, lamps poking out of the heads of plaster sea captains, and a table made out of a ship's wheel.

It was Christmas. We're Jewish, but everyone gets the day off, and Aunt Arlene always goes all out. This year everything was either gold-colored or gold-plated. The tablecloth, candles, silk flower centerpiece, even the flatware was gold. Aunt Arlene wore a gold lamé pantsuit with matching sandals. There wasn't room for everyone at the gold table, so Victor and I ate dinner in the game room, where they keep the billiard table and a full-sized mannequin of an English bobby. We used paper plates and plastic utensils.

During dessert, Aunt Estelle told us about a chip in her sink from the earthquake. They were having to remodel the entire kitchen. "It's impossible to take the sink out without breaking the surrounding tile," she explained. "I've been scrubbing that grout for ten years, so we're going with the granite. It's much more updated."

Victor and I left soon after the presents were opened, drove back to my neighborhood, and took a walk. We passed the house with the arched windows and low roof that makes it look as if it's about ready to sink into the ground. We went by the one with the lighting fixtures everywhere, even on the garage. The people on the corner, they've been landscaping their yard since last summer, and there are big piles of black dirt surrounding their stout cinder block house like an earthbound moat.

We walk by the Neilsons', they have a dark wood sign over the porch that says so. The Neilsons' entire roof and front yard are decorated with huge cardboard figures of Santa Claus, Mickey Mouse, Goofy, Jesus, Mary, and Joseph. A metallic Christmas tree blinks on their lawn.

"Thanks for going with me," I say to Victor.

"Where'd you come from, April?" he asks.

"I don't know," I whisper, "I don't know." It's cold, and I begin to shiver. Victor holds me close as we walk.

Resolution

THIS MILLENNIUM BUSINESS is starting to get to me, and it's still another year away, two depending on who's counting. Last night I dreamed the world ended.

"How did it happen?" Victor asked. We lay side by side on our stomachs, arms pillowing our heads.

"Remote control. People were fooling around with the buttons, and out of boredom, someone flicked the channel. It was sort of anticlimactic, really. Nothing blew up, like how it is in the movies. Everything beautiful just kind of shriveled and faded away. People and animals, the moon, trees. Gradually, the picture got fuzzy, like a TV with lost reception."

"They say dreams can be another facet of yourself," Victor said, nuzzling his elbow against mine.

I leaned over to kiss him between the shoulder blades. "Maybe it's time to trade in my antenna."

Rooted

VICTOR'S TAKEN TO DIGGING in our garden plot. He takes out all the rocks, piles them up in rows. He's getting the soil ready. He has me keeping a little compost bucket at home under the sink. Once a week, he dumps it out into a big plastic garbage container and moves everything around with a pitchfork. When the stuff turns black, he puts it in the ground.

He looks as if he's gardened for years, but he says he doesn't know any more than I do, he's just more willing not to care if anything actually grows. He pulls out the weeds by hand. "What about the roots," I ask, "won't they sprout up again?"

He takes a shovel, digs the earth all around. He tosses big pieces of root into the back of the truck. There's dirt everywhere, and Victor's nails are filthy, but he doesn't care. "That's what soap is for," he says.

One night I tried this recipe from the *Sunset Easy Basics for Good Cooking* that Aunt Dora had brought as a housewarming present. It was for a soup made entirely of root vegetables, carrots, potatoes, turnips, beets. The beets turned the whole thing magenta, it was like some kind of fairy-tale princess potion.

Heart

LIBBY'S BIRTHDAY IS THE DAY after Valentine's. We were sitting in her new kitchen, huddled over a box of See's. We had a butter knife and were cutting open each piece to see what was inside. We were being civilized. When we shared a place, we used to just bite in and put back the ones we didn't like. If we got desperate, we'd suck the chocolate on the leftovers in the box, spitting out the fillings, orange or coconut or raspberry.

"Every year, my dad used to bring me this big, heart-shaped box of chocolates," Libby says, passing me the knife. "I used to think I was the luckiest girl in the world until I realized every other kid got hers the day before. This arrived yesterday UPS, can you believe it? He really planned in advance."

There's a See's factory next to the shop on La Cienega, and if you drive past at the right time, the whole boulevard smells of toffee.

Someone sent my mother a fancy two-pound box after Wilson died, but it was a disappointing assortment, lots of white chocolate and divinity fudge. My mother said it looked like an old-lady box. She threw it right out.

When I was growing up and even before that, my mother kept a heart-shaped tin in the bottom drawer of her nightstand. Sometimes she would open it and lay out the contents. There was her junior high class picture, autograph book, night school diploma. The box that contained my mother before she was my mother, before she was a wife, when she was still a girl, ready to make her life.

The February I was six, there was an earthquake. My mother had a bad flu, the only time I can remember her sick. She had a high fever. We both had fevers. My father had brought her flowers, white and pink carnations with sprays of fern and baby's breath. They flew off her night-stand. The vase was a round glass bulb with a scalloped opening. The glass cracked and all the water leaked out.

Even when we still lived in the same house, my father always sent my valentine through the mail. He knew I loved receiving letters, and finding his card in the box was like a secret conspiracy between us, as if we didn't know each other and someone in the outside world was sending me messages from afar.

Hugo and Victor walked in when they heard Libby and I laughing. They examined all our disregarded choices. "*Mmmm*, coconut," they exclaimed, sharing a neatly cut piece between them.

Fuel

"MY MOM'S GOT A BOYFRIEND," I tell Libby. "He owns a self-service gas station. She helps him out on weekends. She doesn't pump gas or anything, that's all done with credit cards. She works the register in the mini-mart, stocks inventory, makes the place look good."

"Did you check him out yet?" she asks. "What does Victor think?"

"Yeah, we met for dinner last week. He's got kind eyes. He's over the moon about her."

"That's to be expected," Libby says. "Your mom's a looker."

"Well, he's financially savvy, anyway. He owns the place, the land underneath, the whole corner. They keep each other company. I'm happy for her."

"That's great," Libby agrees. "It really is."

"Besides," I add, "she gets her gas for free."

Rhubarb

I HAVE THIS HABIT OF showing Victor all the produce I buy at the supermarket. Sundays I get there by early afternoon, the selection is still good. Victor comes over in the evening, and I sit him down and pull out all the best purchases. Tiny red-skinned potatoes, slender Japanese eggplant, artichokes, full and heavy with sharp, pointed leaves.

I noticed the rhubarb last week, the long stalks poking out of the bin like strange, shocking pink celery. I wasn't quite sure what to do with it, how to choose it, even. I had cut an article out of the newspaper last spring, had filed it away. I was pretty sure it said rhubarb made great pie. "Excuse me," I asked the men who were stacking cauliflower, "do you know how much rhubarb you need for a pie?" They looked blankly at each other, shrugged their shoulders, shook their heads politely.

I stopped an older woman pushing her cart. "Excuse me, do you know anything about rhubarb?" She puckered up like she didn't like rhubarb.

"No," she said.

I put four stalks into a plastic bag and placed them in my basket.

The leeks were in the same row. I had no idea what to

do with those either, but they were fantastic, their green leaves stretched out like fans. I took three, all different sizes.

By the time I got to the checkout, my basket was full: five ears of corn, a bag of radishes, a pound of carrots, five apples, three oranges, two heads of lettuce—butter and red leaf— an orange pepper, three onions, one basket of mushrooms, a quarter-cut cantaloupe, two lemons, and an avocado. The bill was $92.47. I had some non-produce items, too.

Victor came over for dinner later, but I was too tired to cook. He made us quesadillas. He used the avocado. He boiled water for the corn.

"How long does corn take?" I asked. Neither of us knew, so I looked it up in *Sunset Easy Basics*. It said three to five minutes. It said corn was a summer vegetable. We ate cross-legged on the floor at the coffee table.

"I would have predicted you'd be a random corn eater," Victor said, watching me gnaw around the cob.

After dinner, I showed him the leeks, the rhubarb, the waxy orange pepper. "Aren't they beautiful?" I asked.

He laughed and touched them very gently.

"I'm going to make a pie and some soup."

"That's what you keep saying."

Late the next afternoon, I dug out the newspaper article on rhubarb. *Cut into half-inch pieces to make four cups, dredge with a heaping cup of sugar and one-quarter cup of flour, and sprinkle with ground ginger.* It all looked a little dry and bitter, and I didn't have any ginger so I added some juice from the oranges. *Add flakes of butter, cover with a lid, and bake as usual.* I'd never made pie, I didn't know what was usual. I called Libby.

"How do you cook pie, I mean usually?" I asked her.

"I don't usually cook pie. Why don't you call your mom?"

"Libby, if my mom made pie, I'd know what to do already," I said. "Listen, I have the recipe, I just don't know how long to bake it or what temperature."

"What kind of recipe is that?"

"Rhubarb," I said.

"Rhubarb?" I could hear her puckering up over the phone.

"What's wrong with rhubarb?" I asked, adding another cup of sugar to the mixture.

"Nothing," she said. "Try three-fifty for an hour, I think that's what you do for Bundt cakes."

Sunset Easy Basics had a recipe for leek and potato soup, but it didn't call for a pepper. I cut it up and threw it in anyway. It also said to use only the white part of the leeks, but it seemed a shame to waste the pretty green leaves so I added those, too. I didn't have any potatoes.

I finished everything about an hour after Victor got there. Pepper seeds, orange peel, and the skins of onions filled the sink. I turned on the garbage disposal, and the familiar sound of spoons grinding up startled me like it always does. There was flour everywhere.

We ate the soup with my serrated spoons. Hard bits of leek caught like splinters in our mouths. We spit them out into our napkins. "Whoa, killer soup," Victor remarked. "Pretty color, though. I like the little orange and green flecks." He got up from the table, walked over to the refrigerator, took out tortillas, Jack cheese, and the rest of the avocado. "Want a quesadilla?" he asked.

I cut open the pie. Deep red liquid oozed out, leaving a hollow crust and squishy pieces of pale pink fruit. "Maybe we should use bowls?" Victor suggested, opening one of the upper cabinets. "Hey, I remember these." They were the stoneware bowls I'd bought at the Japanese market the day of the earthquake, the ones with the swirls inside.

"Have any ice cream?" he asked.

"In the freezer. Vanilla bean."

He scooped large spoonfuls onto each of our portions. "It's really good, April," he said. "Sweeter than I would have thought."

Shift

I T WAS WILSON WHO took me to the DMV for my driver's test. He taught me how to parallel park, how to change a flat, how to maneuver a stick shift on hills. "Use the emergency brake until your foot feels the clutch engage," he told me. "Remember to turn your wheels when you park."

The whole time he and my mother were married, Wilson drove Pontiac Firebirds. He made a living scouting locations, and his client list ran him all over Los Angeles, so he tore through a Firebird every few years. I watched him negotiate once at the dealership. He wrote down a number on a slip of paper, slid it over to the salesman, said, "My wife says no higher."

"You got it, sir."

Right before the B210 died, he told me to meet him Thursday night after work at one of the big car lots on Ventura Boulevard. "Nobody is going to take that thing as a trade-in," said my mother.

"You never know when luck will be on your side," Wilson said.

He was spot-on about the luck all right, it was St. Patrick's Day, and everyone wanted to get out of there early.

We got the deal of the century, and I drove myself back to Mar Vista in a sporty new Civic, manual transmission, rear disc brakes, power side mirrors, moonroof with tilt, cruise control, clock.

Register

IBBY AND HUGO REGISTERED at this high-end house-wares store. Or rather, Libby and I registered there. Hugo didn't want any part of it. You go in, fill out a form, walk around with a wedding sales associate, trying to coordinate forks, knives, plates, napkins, all the stuff you never needed before you were married. They enter it into this new computerized system so procrastinators like Victor and me can purchase a gift last-minute without saddling anyone with duplicates. Which is how we found ourselves at the mall two days before Libby and Hugo's wedding. That, and I still needed shoes to match my dress.

We take the escalator up from the parking lot, consult the mall directory, and head over to the first of five shoe stores. I pick out some strappy sandals, and while I am trying them on, Victor brings over a pair of urban hiking boots, soft black nubuck with cushioned soles and solid ankle support. "Lotta hills in San Francisco," he says.

The boots feel like magic slippers after the sandals, so I buy them and wear them out of the store. They're so springy, they propel my feet forward, no half steps. "How do you like my new boots?" I ask Victor, clicking the heels together.

"No place like home," he says.

We make our way over to the computer registry that indexes all the couples who will be tying the knot in the next six months. We forget that Libby is short for Elizabeth, and so it takes three attempts to call up her name. We touch the letters on the screen over and over again until it spits out five pages of merchandise.

The list is organized in the following categories: kitchenware, cookware, cutlery, glass, flatware, accessories, table linens, stemware, barware, luggage, and basics. Listed under basics is a wine rack: 12 bottle, natural, $22.95, wants 1, has 1, item# 197-461.

Victor and I go in search of still-available gifts. My new boots keep catching on the display rugs, and it's tricky to maneuver stops by the corners of stacked glass. Finally, we arrive safely at the kitchenware section, where we find white melamine bowls, 14 oz., 4.75" dia. × 2.75" h., item# 628-440. We imagine all the chocolate ice cream we'll be eating over the next forty years in those bowls at Libby and Hugo's, all the strawberry shortcake, the summer red gazpacho.

We carry a dozen up to the counter, and the clerk wraps each ten-dollar-and-fifty-cent bowl as if it were crafted of gold, places them in a cardboard box marked with big black letters, and tapes it all up to go. Victor takes the bag, takes my hand to keep me walking forward, and leads me in my new black boots with the cushioned soles out of the store.

Architecture

LIBBY AND HUGO WERE getting married in Sausalito, at an elegant, historic Craftsman just outside San Francisco.

Wilson had grown up there, by the Marina, it's where he got his start. He used to tell me about his first apartment, a cramped bachelor near Russian Hill. "It had a Murphy bed, and if the mattress was folded up and you hadn't eaten breakfast yet, you could just about turn around, but on a clear day, you could see all the way to the water, and it felt like a million bucks."

Not long after he married my mother, Wilson took us on a road trip, Jake and I tucked into the backseat of the Firebird. At the Golden Gate Bridge, he had us roll down all the windows. *Welcome to the most magnificent structure on the West Coast*, he announced, as if he were a tour guide.

I still had his ashes stashed away in my closet. The woman at the crematorium had told me it was illegal to scatter them, but I figured I'd take my chances. Victor picked me up just after dawn, and we started the drive north.

Rest Stop

ON THE WAY UP, we stop in Pleasanton to visit Esther and Saul, cousins of my father's, the only relatives of his alive. They've been married fifty-three years. They are happy to see us. They've got crackers and cheese, chocolate babka, and Lipton iced tea.

"Maybe you'll catch the bouquet," Esther says, pouring iced tea into orange juice glasses and cutting into the babka. "Nuts, it's still frozen inside," she says.

"Never mind," says Saul. "We've got those fortune cookies from when the kids took us out for Chinese last week. They're still wrapped."

"Look at April's waist," Esther remarks. "I used to have a waist like that."

I ask Esther about her heart.

"I don't know," she sighs, "maybe I was expecting too much, but I'm tired all the time. It wasn't a bypass, you know. Those are easy. What they did, they replaced two valves in my heart. They're plastic. During the day, I don't notice it, but at night when I'm in bed, I can hear them working, click-click, click-click."

"That must take some getting used to," Victor says, and Esther says, "That's exactly right."

Saul offers me a cookie. I press it out of the cellophane and read the fortune inside:

Stop searching forever, happiness is just next to you.

Promise

IT'S A BEAUTIFUL WEDDING. Libby is stunning, and Hugo looks good, too, in the tuxedo that came free with her gown. Victor and I are the only attendants, and we don't mess it up. Victor has the ring ready at the right time, I hold the flowers upright. Libby and Hugo exchange vows under an oak tree, and after the ceremony, Libby's parents host an impeccable lunch reception: garden salad with baby lettuce, roasted new potatoes, poached salmon, roast lamb with mint. The cake is chocolate raspberry with whipped cream filling. There is music and dancing. Someone catches the bouquet, then places it in my hands when no one's looking.

Bridge

I HELD WILSON'S ASHES in my arms. The box was heavy with death.

"Victor, I get afraid," I said, my throat catching. "Afraid I won't want to live, like my dad."

"I understand," he said. He reached his arm around me and turned his body to shield me from the wind. "Truly, I do."

We were standing on the bridge, looking down. The current ran fast. Tears wet my face.

He took the ashes from my hands, set them on the ground. "April," he said, lifting my chin and touching the nape of my neck. His palm was warm. "You are so loved. And we're here. Libby and Hugo. Your mom. Jake and Emily. The Joes, the aunts. Me." He placed his hands on my shoulders, kissed me on the forehead, the eyes, the lips, each cheek. "Don't be afraid, April. I promise, you'll come around again."

I saw us standing there from above, the wind blowing, the sadness pressing in, the missing of Wilson and my father, and always, it seemed, the end of love. I saw it clearly now, a snapshot taken with Wilson's camera of a boat down below, sailing by with all the love in the world and all the loss on board, and my throat caught again, and my heart waked open like the water parting the bow.

We cast Wilson's ashes into the bay, emptied the box to the sky. They blew out, and all the hope that ever was. I tried to imagine what happens to hope that's mixed with ash. Would it fly in circles forever, or would it someday land again? I missed them then, the tears were salty in my mouth, Wilson and my father, and I was thinking of the future, and I was crying hard. I had two fathers who loved me. That's more than most. Then Victor pulled me to him, and led me gently off the bridge.

Watchspring

WILSON HAD THIS WATCH, it had a slender silver-link band and a flat white face with elegant black Roman numerals. Until he and my mother married, I'd never seen a watch that thin. It sat almost undetected on his wrist, but it must have worked because he never seemed late or rushed. He used to wait patiently for my mother in the car while she took her time saying goodbye to the aunts at family gatherings.

There's this article I read in the newspaper about how watching something can make it change. Apparently, they did this experiment where they measured molecules. They had people watch the molecules, and then they measured again and found that they had changed in some way, shape or weight, or something inside.

According to this research, something as minor as taking pictures changes the world, at least on a molecular level. I wonder what would happen if a person couldn't see for whatever reason, or if there was absolute darkness.

When Wilson was dying, I'd stay at the hospital all day in the sticky vinyl chair by his bed. I'd read him the sports section. There was a big clock on the wall. I held his hand five hours straight one day. I read a *People* magazine of Aunt Arlene's over and over again so he'd think I was

doing something besides waiting. About every thirty minutes, he'd open his eyes.

"Am I still alive?" he'd ask, surprised.

Vision

I OPENED MY BOX of photos for Victor. There were the shots from Fourth of July, Solstice Canyon, Libby and Hugo's wedding, the view from the garden.

"These are good, April. Really good. Why don't you have a show?"

"That's what Libby is always asking. She says I should poach names off the museum-donor Rolodex for the invite list."

"Do it," says Victor. "I can build shadow-box frames if you want."

I had this professor in art school, and whenever you'd see her, she'd have this battered Olympus across her chest. She believed that whenever we took a picture, we were doing more than just capturing, we were bringing something new into being, composing the frame. "Sculpture, writing, photography. Something might still exist if you didn't, but it wouldn't be exactly the same. Your version wouldn't have been made. It's action that creates what we're looking at now. Something out of nothing, see?"

"A show would be great," I say. "How about let's start with an album, include the dates and everything."

Go

WE DRIVE A LOT. We don't go anywhere in particular, we just drive. Or so it seems. To tell the real truth, Victor does the driving. I sit in the passenger seat and watch the white line on the side of the road.

Victor's got this 1976 Toyota truck, an SR5 longbed with over 172,000 miles on it, and it seems like we add another five hundred miles every weekend, driving around, trying to get from one place to another. The body's all right if you don't mind avocado green, but being in the cab is like sitting inside an emptied-out vacuum cleaner bag, you can see the dust floating around in the glare. Late in the evening, it gets pretty cold from the air blowing in the broken back window. The middle of the steering wheel is smashed from where Victor put his fist through it before we met. Argos's collar hangs from the rearview mirror, his gold tag like some Saint Christopher medallion, patron saint of travelers.

We've gotten pulled over a few times. The officer gives Victor a fix-it ticket while he's waiting to find out if the truck is stolen. Then he comes round to my side to see if I'm all right, if I'm there of my own free will.

It takes about twenty minutes to go anywhere in Los Angeles, not including parking. I'm no mathematician, but if you've got three errands to run, that's a slow hour in traffic, not including the errands themselves, which, in addition to the time involved, always cost money. If you sleep late, you may as well tack on an extra fifteen minutes to each trip. Victor and I, we always sleep late.

Sometimes, after we've spent a dusty Saturday afternoon in the truck, I have this dream. I'm driving on a long curved freeway overpass, and when I get to the deepest part of the arc, I drive clear off the asphalt, into the air. I don't lose control of the car or anything, I don't even crash through the retaining wall. I just miss the curve and keep driving straight until I realize that I'm not on the road anymore, that there's nothing beneath the wheels. That always wakes me up.

Most trips, we take my car. I have a white Honda Civic, very practical. It's about four years old, Wilson picked it out right before my B210 fell apart. I make the monthly payments. Lately, though, we've needed a truck. There's been a lot of moving, a lot of hauling.

I once read a list of ten things that cause the most stress for people: death, divorce, marriage, moving. I don't remember the rest, but last year there were two deaths, three moves, four boyfriends, three breakups, one earthquake, and not nearly enough money to make up for it all. There was also an engagement and a wedding, neither of them mine, just like the fortune-teller predicted.

I needed vacation, no adventure, just a vacation. No driving. I wanted to sit on warm white sand until I got bored. I started cutting ads out of the Sunday *Times*. My refrigerator was plastered with them. Maui for thirty-three dollars a month: eight days including plane fare, garden-view room, continental breakfast, orientation, fresh flower lei greeting, transfers, taxes, and a tote bag. It seemed like a good deal, but neither Victor nor I had thirty-three dollars.

All the pictures in the magazine advertising supplements made the Hawaiian water seem so blue, so warm, so inviting. They showed people swimming, snorkeling, scuba diving. Underwater coral forests and strangely striped fish.

I was driving home from the museum, listening to National Public Radio. They were talking about this tiny instrument that tells you exactly where you are anywhere on earth, longitude and latitude, within a couple of meters. It's called a Global Positioning System. Apparently, there are these satellites in the sky that figure out all the math and then tell you where you are. I don't know how this would help a person, exactly. I already know where I am, and I'm not in Hawaii.

The next day, I got a letter from the local public radio station. They know I've been listening all year for free, it was about their subscription-drive sweepstakes. One of the prizes was a weeklong stay in Hawaii. *Enjoy the serenity of your own private lanai, the beauty of luxurious grounds perfumed by gardens of the tropics, and the tranquillity of unspoiled white-sand beaches.* I sent in five dollars and wondered how many times we could get to Hawaii on 172,000 miles.

My mother went once, the only time she spent a night without Wilson until he died. She went with the aunts, they saved up for months. Aunt Estelle fell asleep the instant they reached the hotel. "What's the matter with you?" my mother demanded. Turns out the doctor had given her a prescription the day before they'd left. My mother flushed the Benadryl down the toilet and said, "Too bad about your ringworm. I didn't come all the way to Hawaii to sit in a hotel room." They were there a week. Aunt Estelle came home, her body covered with red circles.

Libby and Hugo are there now, in Oahu, on their honeymoon. Victor is remodeling their bathroom while they are gone, and we are driving back from the Valley. The fog is settling in the pass.

"Keep your eye on the white line," Wilson used to tell me, and always, driving at night or in a thick fog, on a deeply curved freeway overpass, I've followed his advice.

Victor and I are deep in the mountains now. We can see the Getty with its imported stone and sophisticated lighting. "Victor," I say suddenly, "how do you drive in low visibility?"

Not taking his eyes off the road, he replies, "Look for the white line. Otherwise you get blinded from the lights of the oncoming cars."

As we approach the off-ramp for Mar Vista, the cool night air blows in through the window. There is no dust in the darkness.

Victor's truck got stolen, of course. A truck gets to be that old, and it's just a matter of time before it gets taken. This year seemed right. We'd been out, working in the garden, when they left this message: "We found your truck. Someone crashed it into a tree. It's been towed to the LAPD holding yard."

It costs $150 to get it out, and miles of driving. Off the new Century Freeway, out in the middle of nowhere, nothing but gas plants and used auto-parts shops, down a narrow pitted driveway to a chain-link fence topped with circles of barbed wire. The place is a dirt lot filled with cars in various stages of disrepair—no tires, hoods missing, engines gone. A guard is sitting outside in a lounge chair next to a portable building that serves as the office. His head is shaved bare except for a tiny braid at the nape of his neck, and he's wearing a heavy jacket because it can get cold in March, even in Los Angeles.

He takes Victor and me over to the truck, but the engine won't turn over, so Victor crawls underneath while I wait in the Honda and watch the planes take off over LAX. We are under the flight path. They go fast, one after the other, it's a busy place.

"I like watching them, too," the guard says to me through the open window of the Honda. "I sit in my chair and look over all night. It makes the time go."

"I guess it does," I say, and then, wondering, "Ever been to Hawaii?"

"Naw, shit," he says.

We look up at the sky. In another night, the moon will be full. The lights of the planes blink in the end-of-winter darkness, and Victor pulls himself up from under the truck. "It needs a new starter," he says.

"Hey, why don't you just come back tomorrow?" offers the guard. "I'm here until seven, they won't know about the extra day."

"Hey, thanks, I'll see you then," Victor says, as he climbs into the passenger side of my car, pressing dirt into the seat.

"Thanks for waiting, April," he says, kissing me, and then, "I love you. Let's go."

And I drive through the gate and onto the dusty road, where there is no white line, and my eyes look up to see the white lights of the planes. They make a trail, and we drive, and we drive, and we drive, until we drive straight off the high overpass of the Century Freeway, through the air and into the Pacific, where the water washes over us until, finally, we are swimming with the striped fish in the deep, blue ocean.

Acknowledgments

The existence of this book is the result of an entire universe of encouragement, for which I am deeply grateful. Long-standing thanks to its earliest champions: Claudette Brown, Lynn Melnick, Amy Tan, Rick Wartzman, the James Jones Literary Society, the Community of Writers at Squaw Valley, and the kindest of inspirers, Jim Krusoe, who counseled all those years ago: *keep writing*.

More recent, albeit endless, gratitude to the constellation of luminaries at Melville House who launched *Death and Other Holidays* into the world and gave it such an elegant and graceful form: Dennis Johnson, Valerie Merians, Susan Rella, Marina Drukman, Betty Lew, and Michael Barron, editor above and beyond. Heartfelt thanks, as well, to Rivka Galchen, for generous good will.

For detecting starlight in an unknown manuscript, I thank Jim Shepard and the extraordinary support of the Miami Book Fair and The de Groot Foundation. Especial thanks to Clydette de Groot, whose phone call transformed an ordinary autumn afternoon into a perennial holiday.

A galaxy of thanks to treasured mentors and comrades at the University of Southern California: Aimee Bender, Janalynn Bliss, Heather Dundas, Percival Everett, Susan McCabe, and David St. John.

For steadfast companionship, protection, and essential walks: Tang, Chado, and Argon, the original brown dog. To cherished friends, thank you for circling the calendar together, year in and year out. To Peter, always—thank you for being on the same planet.

To my family, close and extended: I love you to the moon and back.